ALICE IN WONDERLAND

**Dramatized
by
William Glennon**

The Dramatic Publishing Company
Woodstock, Illinois • London, England • Melbourne, Australia

*** NOTICE ***

The amateur and stock acting rights to this work are controlled exclusively by THE DRAMATIC PUBLISHING COMPANY without whose permission in writing no performance of it may be given. Royalty fees are given in our current catalogue and are subject to change without notice. Royalty must be paid every time a play is performed whether or not it is presented for profit and whether or not admission is charged. A play is performed anytime it is acted before an audience. All inquiries concerning amateur and stock rights should be addressed to: THE DRAMATIC PUBLISHING COMPANY, 311 Washington St., Woodstock, Illinois 60098.

COPYRIGHT LAW GIVES THE AUTHOR OR HIS AGENT THE EXCLUSIVE RIGHT TO MAKE COPIES.

This law provides authors with a fair return for their creative efforts. Authors earn their living from the royalties they receive from book sales and from the performance of their work. Conscientious observance of copyright law is not only ethical, it encourages authors to continue their creative work. This work is fully protected by copyright. No alterations, deletions or substitutions may be made in the work without the prior written consent of the publisher. No part of this work may be reproduced or transmitted in any form or by any means, electronic or mechanical, including photocopy, recording, videotape, film, or any information storage and retrieval system, without permission in writing from the publisher. It may not be performed either by professionals or amateurs without payment of royalty. All rights, including but not limited to the professional, motion picture, radio, television, videotape, foreign language, tabloid, recitation, lecturing, publication, and reading are reserved. On all programs this notice should appear: "Produced by special arrangement with THE DRAMATIC PUBLISHING COMPANY of Woodstock, Illinois."

©MCMLXXXV by
WILLIAM GLENNON
Revised ©MCMXCI
Printed in the United States of America
All Rights Reserved
(ALICE IN WONDERLAND)

ISBN 0-87129-063-4

Cover Design by Susan Carle.

ALICE IN WONDERLAND

A Play in Two Acts
For 9-13 Actors

CHARACTERS

ALICE
WHITE RABBIT
THE MOUSE
FISH FOOTMAN
FROG FOOTMAN
THE DUCHESS
THE COOK
THE CHESHIRE CAT
MARCH HARE
DORMOUSE
THE HATTER
KING OF HEARTS
QUEEN OF HEARTS
KNAVE OF HEARTS
THE GRYPHON
MOCK TURTLE
TWO PLAYING CARDS

The production requires props, not scenery, and can be played against a neutral background or lighted cyc.

TO THE PRODUCER:

Originally this script was written to be performed by eight actors as the "Wonderland Group" plus Alice. However, in the first production, I used thirteen, plus Alice. (One actor played the Mouse, the March Hare, and the Mock Turtle; Fish Footman and Frog Footman doubled as the Playing Cards during the croquet game; the Dormouse and the Gryphon were doubled. Further doubling is possible and in keeping with the original intent).

The actors should be numbered for the roll call in the opening and lines distributed as desired, with Number One more or less in charge. Group activity, however, is the basic idea—much like the *Commedia d'elle Arte*—a planned outline filled with spontaneous moments.

Our company carried a few props on with them, and found the others in the wings. Placards, for example, were carried. They were decorated with question marks, exclamation points, and patterns, to arouse curiosity. Later they doubled as the opening to the garden and the door to the kitchen. For the croquet game we used short sections of a picket fence as a "boundary" and the stools seen earlier were turned over so roses could be inserted in the holes drilled in the legs. The fence went on to make a witness box for the trial which also had small ladders instead of thrones for the King and Queen. We had a stylized stove in the kitchen scene and a coat rack big enough for the Cheshire Cat to curl up on, but mostly the "scenery" was sparse.

Our company wore tights and collared smocks to begin with. Midway through Act One nearly everyone was in full costume. Suggestions of the costume would be just fine, though. That approach goes along with the idea of spontaneity and inventiveness, whatever it takes to help Alice—and the audience—enjoy her "turn."

William Glennon

ACT ONE

SCENE: *The ACTORS enter through the house as the lights dim. As they walk down the aisles, they are talking with each other about their predicament. Anxious to do "Alice in Wonderland," they have found they lack an Alice. They have all opted for the other parts it seems. The audience hears snatches of their exchanges.*

ACTOR. Imagine. Without the White Rabbit, yes. We could skip that part. The Mock Turtle, you bet. Cut that scene. But no Alice? Impossible.

ACTOR. Why didn't you agree to be Alice?

ACTOR. Because.

ACTOR. Because why?

ACTOR. Same reason as you. I like my own part.

ACTOR. Well, it's not "The Mad Hatter in Wonderland" or "The Queen of Hearts in Wonderland." It's "Alice in Wonderland." *(Etc.)*

ONE *(LEADER, now at front of house near apron)*. Now, now, now. We've got a little stumbling block, true, but we've been in worse pickles.

TWO. Name one. *(ACTORS are now sitting on apron, leaning on it, standing on edge of stage, etc.)*

ONE. Well, let's see.

TWO. You can't do "Alice in Wonderland" without an Alice. So let's give up. *(ACTOR with highest number suddenly discovers the slit in curtain. He's curious and slips through.)*

ONE. Perhaps someone's reconsidered. That's a possibility. Let's count off again.

TWO. We've counted off and counted off and counted off and we're still in the same pickle. It's not a possibility.

FIVE. Actually we're in a theatre.

SIX. Good place for a story.

TWO. We're in a pickle in a theatre and there isn't going to be a story. Face it.

ONE. Now, now. Let's hear it! Count off! I'll start things rolling. One! *(And he names the part he's going to play.)*

TWO *(unhappy)*. Two. *(And his part. The roll call continues until all the parts have been named with the exception of the ACTOR who went in back of curtain.)* See? We may as well pack up and go home. No Alice, and that's that.

SEVEN. No Wonderland.

EIGHT. Bother.

ONE. Aren't we missing a part?

TWO. Of course! Alice! How many times must you be told?

ONE. No, someone else...

(ACTOR returns from behind curtain. He is excited.)

ACTOR. Listen!

ONE. Oh, yes, there he is. And you're going to be...uh...

ACTOR. Listen. There's a girl. *(Giggles.)* A girl. Just behind this thing. *(Curtain.)* And she's sitting there doing nothing.

ONE. Nothing?

ACTOR. Well, daydreaming, maybe.
ONE. That sounds promising.
ACTOR. And she's young and pretty and just perfect for you-know-who. *(A murmer.)*
TWO. But she's not one of us.
ACTOR. Well, she could be, couldn't she?
TWO. But she won't know what to do.
ACTOR. That's never stopped you.
ONE. Now, now, now. Mustn't bicker.
ACTOR. Come on. See for yourself.
FIVE. We could help her, you know, along the way. We know what to do. Sort of.
ONE. She can certainly help us.
ACTOR. Let's give it a go! Shall we?
ONE. Well, I see no reason why we can't at least *look* at her.
FOUR. No reason at all. So let's look.
TWO. How do we get rid of this thing? *(Curtain.)*
ONE. Blow it away.

(ALL take in deep breaths and blow. The curtain rises. ALICE is seated center, daydreaming. They seem to like her. Quietly they tiptoe from the house to the stage, passing far right and left. As they move, ALICE speaks and ALL freeze.)

ALICE. What a lazy day. With nothing to do. Perhaps I should have followed my sister when she left. "Come along. Back to the house and I'll fix you some tea. Don't you want some tea, Alice?" *(ALL heads turn quickly to her. They are amazed.)* "Not yet, dear sister. I'm going to stay here a for a while. By the stream. In the sunshine. I'll have my tea later, thank you." *(She *sighs. They look at each other, bright-eyed.)* Oh, I do wish something unusual would happen. *(ALL snort softly and move quietly to set up necessary props.)* Something *very* unusual.

ACTOR. Unusual!
ACTOR *(as they place stools around ALICE)*. And fun.
ACTOR. Can't wait!
ONE. Ready?
ACTOR. Ready.

(ONE mounts a stool at UL, raises his arm with extended finger and then drops finger as a signal to begin. ALICE doesn't quite hear the following but senses something.)

FIVE. The White Rabbit hurries for fear he'll be late...
EIGHT. Imagine his fate if he makes the Queen wait!
SIX. Down in the ground where the hole goes so deep...
THREE. The tumble is liable to put you to sleep. *(ALL giggle.)*
THIRTEEN. You'll fall at a speed that will make your ears sing,
ONE. Past curious whatchamacallits and things,
EIGHT. Past orange marmalade in a jar on the shelf,
TEN. Past mirrors that smile when you smile at yourself. *(ALL giggle.)*
SIX. Past odd little doors and a window or two,
FIVE. Perhaps you'll encounter a picture of you!
THIRTEEN. Down deeper and deeper and deeper you'll go,
SIX. Down deep in the rabbit hole, head over toe;
THREE. You'll fall to a place so unusually gay,
EIGHT. It's terribly likely you'll hear yourself say:

ONE. It's bewitching, beloved, beyootiful and...
ALL. Grand,
ONE. So wondrously wonderful, your...
ALL. Wonderland!
THREE. So becoming, befuddled, beguiling and...
ALL. Grand,
ONE. So wondrously wonderful, your...
ALL. Wonderland! *(They cup hands over faces, open hands and call softly.)* Alice! *(ALICE looks about as if she's almost heard them.)* Alice! *(She smiles.)*

(WHITE RABBIT has donned ears, a waistcoat and has a watch. He now leaps from behind the GROUP.)

ONE. Now.
RABBIT *(hops DL)*. Oh my ears and whiskers, I'll be late!
ALICE. Sitting on a wooded bank, one can occasionally expect a white rabbit to scamper by. Curious though, when the white rabbit is wearing a waistcoat, carrying a watch and is able to speak. Late? Late for what?
RABBIT. Now where's the hole? I must find the hole! It will never do to keep the Duchess waiting.
ACTOR. That's my part!
ACTOR. Sh!
RABBIT. Oh, my dear little paws and fur, I can't find the hole! If I'm late getting home, I'll be late for the Duchess, and if I'm late for the Duchess, I'll be late for the Queen's croquet game. And if I'm late for the Queen's croquet game she'll chop off my head!

(The OTHERS have formed a human "rabbit hole" at left, with signs identifying it as such. One says "Rabbit

Hole," the other, "Enter Here." They get these props from the wings—or perhaps have carried them on.)

TWO *(holding sign "Enter Here")*. Ahem!
RABBIT. Bless my whiskers. Here's the hole! *(He enters the "hole.")*
THREE. Do you think she'll follow?
ALICE. I think I'll follow. *(Rises and crosses to hole.)*
ONE. I think she'll follow.
ALICE. Odd. I never noticed this rabbit hole before. *(The OTHERS form a tunnel above the hole.)* Very curious. *(Reading signs.)* "Rabbit Hole." "Enter Here." Well... I'm not exactly a rabbit, but...*(She enters.)*
SIX. There she goes!

(The "tunnel" moves, with ALICE inside it, to center, where it becomes the circular wall of the hole through which ALICE is falling. The actors face ALICE in a tight circle, their arms over their heads.)

THREE. Down deeper and deeper and deeper she'll go.
ONE. Down deep in the rabbit hole, head over toe.
ALICE *(rising and swaying, as though she is falling as the OTHERS kneel)*. I must be nearly to the center of the earth. *(They rise again and she drops out of sight.)*
TEN. She'll fall at a speed that'll make her ears sing...
TWO. Past curious whatchamacallits and things...
ALICE *(rising)*. I keep falling past the most curious things...
SIX. Past orange marmalade in a jar on the shelf...
NINE. Past mirrors that smile when you smile at yourself.
ALICE *(rising)*. A mirror smiled back at me. Nothing curious there, but if I keep falling this way, I shall surely land on the other side of the world where people

Act I   ALICE IN WONDERLAND   Page 11

have to walk on their heads, and that will be extremely curious.

ONE. Is she nearly there?

ACTOR. Almost!

ALICE *(rising)*. I wonder what Dinah, my cat, would think of all this. Such a fall, I dare say, would probably cause her hair to stand on end. What's the White Rabbit going to be late *for*? The Duchess? A croquet game?

RABBIT. The White Rabbit hurries for fear he'll be late. Imagine his fate if he makes the Queen wait!

ALL. She's almost there. THUMP! *("Hole" splits apart. The ACTORS scatter about.)*

ALICE *(on the floor)*. Didn't hurt at all. When I get home I'm going to fall down the stairs just to show how brave I am.

ALL. Oh?

ALICE. Three stairs to the landing. *(She rises, looks about and crosses DR).* Well, I wonder where I am now. And where's the White Rabbit, I wonder...

ALL *(overlapping her)*. Wonderland...Wonderland... *(They are forming a door at center. See Production Note #1.)*

ALICE *(overlapping)*. I wonder where this goes. *(On hands and knees, looking through tiny doorway.)* Why, there's a garden! *(SEVERAL behind doorway hold up roses.)* A lovely garden...with fountains! *(ACTOR runs to left of door and squirts water.)* But I shall never be able to go through this little doorway. I'm much too big.

ALL. Tsk, tsk, tsk.

ALICE. Oh, dear, what a pity I can't just shut up like a telescope. Considering what's happened so far today, I don't really think shutting up like a telescope is all that impossible. *(She leans on a crate upon which has been placed a little bottle and a sign "Drink Me.")* "Drink Me." Hmmm. Wonder if I should. I seem to be wondering quite a bit today. I wonder...

ALL *(overlapping)*. Wonderland! Wonderland!

ALICE *(overlapping)*. I wonder...Well, it isn't marked "poison" and that's a good sign. It's a sensible rule to avoid anything marked "poison." Yes. Hmmm.

ALL. Hmmm!

ALICE *(rises)*. Just a little bit. *(She drinks.)* Mmmm. Tastes like a mixture of cherry tarts, plum pudding and buttered biscuits.

ALL. Mmmmmm!

ALICE *(drinks)*. Very nice. Very nice, indeed. *(Slide whistle. The door grows larger as ALICE "shrinks.")* Well, here goes the telescope again! Mustn't shut up too far or it might be like a candle going out. And I don't want to go out. Then I'd never get through to that lovely garden. *(The bottle is replaced by a piece of cake with sign "Eat Me.")* "Eat Me!" Oh, I do love currant cake. *(She eats some of the cake and begins to grow as the door grows smaller.)* Well, I never! A bit of currant cake and I'm back to normal size, or maybe even bigger. *(She checks the opening.)* Yes, bigger. Now I shall never get through to the garden. Never, never, never. *(She cries.)* First, I'm as tall as a house, and then I'm as small as a mouse. It's getting curiouser and curiouser. Indeed it is. I must stop crying though, especially since I can't remember why I started. Oh, yes! The dear garden with flowers, *(Garden appears.)* and fountains, *(Fountain appears and squirts water, and shrugs.)* I shall never see. *(She cries again. TWO ACTORS hand her water-soaked handkerchiefs with which she wipes *her eyes and then wrings them out.)* And where's the White Rabbit? How rude of him to vanish. He must have known I was following him. How very rude. Besides, I don't know where I am or where I'm going or how to get there! *(She "shrinks" again; the door grows.)* I'm...I'm...I'm shutting up again! I'm shrinking! And I didn't eat a bite or drink a drop. It must be in my system.

(A long piece of blue silk is taken from the costume of one of the actors. FIVE ACTORS sit on stools placed in a semicircle around two stools and make waves with the long piece of silk, and the other props are taken off.)

ALICE. I must run. I don't know where or why, but I must run! *(She does, until she "slips" and falls into the pool of tears. She is on her knees behind stool at right, with stomach on stool and making swimming gestures with arms. She tastes water.)* Why, it's salt water!

(ONE, wearing mouse ears, "swims" toward her and leans over a stool, "swimming.")

ALICE. Excuse me.
MOUSE. Why? What'd you do?
ALICE. I didn't *do* anything.
MOUSE. Then what do you want to be excused for?
ALICE. I don't want to be excused for anything, really.
MOUSE. In that case, I would advise you not to say "Excuse me." *(He starts away.)*
ALICE. Please don't swim away.
MOUSE. I can't swim in one place.

ALICE *(noticing him for the first time)*. Why, you're a mouse.

MOUSE. No comment.

ALICE. Can you tell me where I am?

MOUSE. You ought to know. They're your tears, not mine.

ALICE. My tears? *(Looks around.)* Amazing.

MOUSE. Big tears, I'd say. You must be quite blubbery.

ALICE. Don't mice cry?

MOUSE. Not this much. It would take me a hundred years to cry a pool this size.

ALICE. I must tell Dinah.

MOUSE. Who's Dinah?

ALICE. Dinah's my dear little cat.

MOUSE. A cat! *(He gasps, holds nose and "dives" under.)*

ALICE. Oh, I'm sorry. I don't suppose we should talk about cats.

MOUSE *(coming up, gasping for breath)*. *I* wasn't.

ALICE. But Dinah's such a sweet pet. I'm sure you'd take a great fancy to her. She purrs *(ALICE purrs.)* and washes her face with her paws, and she's such a great one for catching…uh oh…

MOUSE. She's a serpent! *(He "dives" again.)*

ALICE. I beg your pardon.

MOUSE *(up again)*. Pardon granted.

ALICE. Good. Now how do we get out of here?

MOUSE. Try swimming to shore.

ALICE. What'll I find there?

MOUSE. Depends on which shore you swim to. *(Giggles.)*

ALICE. Well, I'm looking for a white rabbit.

MOUSE. Why?

ALICE. I followed him and poof! he vanished.

MOUSE. A likely story.

ALICE. I believe he was on his way to a croquet game.

MOUSE. That so.

ALICE. You think I should attend the croquet game, too?

MOUSE. Did she invite you?

ALICE. Who?

MOUSE. The Queen.

ALICE. No. But I have a feeling that's where I'm going.

MOUSE. Better see the Duchess first.

ALICE. Where can I find her?

MOUSE. Where she lives, of course. But don't say I told you. I don't care to have *my* head chopped off.

ALICE. Neither do I.

MOUSE. Well, that's what she'll do, you know.

ALICE. Who? The Duchess?

MOUSE. No, the Queen. She's uncommonly fond of beheading people.

ALICE. That's very...rude.

MOUSE. Try telling *her* that.

ALICE. One can't go about chopping people's heads off. It just isn't done.

MOUSE. Just isn't done! *(He swims away and the pool of tears follows him. All stools and props are struck.)*

ALICE. Wait! I've several questions I want to ask you. It's impolite to swim away when I haven't finished...

(RABBIT appears at right.)

RABBIT. Mary Ann! What are you doing in the tub with your clothes on?

ALICE. Mary Ann!?

RABBIT. Don't call me "Mary Ann." I'm not Mary Ann. You're Mary Ann.

ALICE. But...

RABBIT. No "buts" about it. Run home this instant and fetch my white gloves and a fan.

ALICE *(indicating "soaked" dress).* Look, I'm rather wet...

RABBIT. If you run fast enough the wind will dry you off. Quickly! I'm late! I'll need my white gloves for the croquet game...it's one of her new rules...and the fan for the tea party, if she's in the mood. Hurry! *(Crosses to left.)*

ALICE. Which way?

RABBIT *(turns).* Which way? Which way indeed! No idle questions! Off with you! *(Looks at his watch.)* Oh, my wrinkly nose and pointed ears! Look at the time. *(Starts off at left.)* I'll meet you there promptly. *(Turns.)* On the dot! *(He is gone.)*

ALICE. I'm not Mary Ann. I'm Alice, I think. And I haven't the faintest idea where home is, his home or mine. Perhaps if I run far enough, I'll find one of them, though it wouldn't surprise me very much if I didn't. *(She smiles.)* It's like a game without rules.

(As ALICE runs in place, facing left, SEVEN, THIRTEEN and TWELVE run from left to right, one at a time, carrying signs: A TREE, A BUSH, ANOTHER TREE.)

ALICE *(after watching signs).* Everything's so curious, and getting curiouser all the time.

(She "loses" ground, and TEN runs on from left as FISH FOOTMAN. They run toward each other and stop at center.)

FISH (*"acting" grand, but with a twinkle*). You see this handsomely engraved invitation, I suppose?

ALICE. Yes, I do.

FISH. Well, it's not for you. So stop your whining.

ALICE. I beg your pardon.

FISH. That will do no good whatsoever. I'm not in a position to grant pardons.

ALICE. The very idea.

FISH. That's it! The very idea! You seem rather bright but your hair wants cutting.

ALICE. Personal comments are not in very good taste.

FISH. And good taste is just what we'll have when the tarts are ready.

ALICE. What tarts?

FISH (*he hops to other side of her, making fish noises*). I know you know the invitation is for the Duchess to attend the croquet game and have a tart with the Queen afterwards.

ALICE. It is?

FISH. The Queen of Hearts, she made some tarts, all on a summer day! And so forth.

ALICE. Yes, I've heard that before.

FISH. Of course you have...I just said it! If you'd cut your hair you'd hear better. That's only common sense.

ALICE. Has anyone stolen the tarts?

FISH. Not yet. We've got to run. Quickly!

ALICE. Why?

FISH. To stay in the same place!

(*They run in place toward left. THIRTEEN, SEVEN and TWELVE enter right, running. TWELVE carries fancy tops for easels on which placards were placed in house, which are soon to become the double doors to the DUCHESS' house.)*

ALICE. I don't want to stay in the same place, if you don't mind.

FISH. But, I do mind. Faster! *(THIRTEEN and SEVEN break and run to fetch "doors." They construct the doors at upper right.)*

ALICE. We don't seem to be getting anywhere.

FISH. Faster! Faster!

ALICE *(losing ground and backing to DR)*. I do wish we could have a little rest.

FISH *(stops running and ALICE catches up to him DL)*. Stop!

ALICE *(looking about)*. We don't seem to have moved at all. We're in exactly the same place.

FISH. Would you have it otherwise?

ALICE. Well, in my country, when we run fast we generally get somewhere.

FISH. Time for knocks on the door.

ALICE. What door?

FISH. There. *(He goes to door, pantomimes three knocks on door. THIRTEEN and SEVEN, behind doors, say "Knock" each time FISH pantomimes a knock.)*

FISH. Hark ye! Hark ye! Open ye! An invitation from the Queen.

(FROG steps through doors as they are opened.)

FROG. The Frog Footman, servant to the Duchess, at your service.

FISH. The Queen invites the Duchess to a game of croquet and dearly hopes she can make it or else.

FROG. I see. *(Sneezes.)*
ALICE. Bless you.
FISH *(to FROG)*. Pay no attention to her. She's waiting for a haircut.
FROG. It's not her turn.
FISH. I know it, but she kept screaming at me. *(ALICE smiles but sobers when they look at her.)*
FROG *(to ALICE)*. The Duchess is not fond of people who scream. She's highly sensitive to screaming.
ALICE. I didn't scream and I'm not waiting for a haircut.
FISH. Why do you need a haircut?
ALICE. I don't need a haircut.
FISH. See? She makes no sense at all.
FROG. None whatsoever.
ALICE. I think you're trying to confuse me.
FROG. The Duchess is very sensitive to confusion. *(To FISH.)* I'll give her the invitation and pray I don't get hit with a pot.
ALICE. The Duchess might throw a pot at you?
FROG. Of course not. But the cook will. *(FROG, in a series of mechanical motions takes the invitation from the FISH. Then he motions FISH out of the way. The door opens, he waves at ALICE and disappears. All through the preceding, he makes frog noises.)*
ALICE. A strange household, I'd say.
FISH. Please don't expect me to stay. She'll need cherries for the tarts. *(He starts to run backwards.)*
ALICE. If you run that way, you can't see where you're going!
FISH. I know. Makes for surprises. *(He continues backwards.)*
ALICE. Perhaps this is where I'm supposed to meet the White Rabbit on the dot.

(She goes to door. ONE [LEADER] enters and goes to FISH.)

ONE *(loud whisper)*. She's doing just fine, isn't she? And having fun, too.
FISH *(still on the run)*. Wait'll she meets the Duchess.
ONE. And her cook! *(They exit.)*
ALICE *(pantomimes knocking the way FISH did)*. May I come in?

(Lights flash and horrible vocal sounds are heard as ACTORS set scene for DUCHESS' house. See Production Note #2.)

DUCHESS *(singing)*.
> Speak roughly to your little boy,
> And beat him when he sneezes;
> He only does it to annoy,
> Because he knows it teases.

COOK *(rushes to DUCHESS and joins in)*. Wow! Wow! Wow! *(She returns to stove.)*
DUCHESS. I know a million verses to that song and I hate 'em all. *(She sneezes.)*
ALICE. Bless you. *(COOK places a pot over her head, hits it with another, and sinks behind the stove.)* Well, I never!
DUCHESS. Living backwards, that's what does it. *(The BABY cries violently. It is VOICE of an ACTOR off left.)* What's the matter with you? Want a good bouncing? *(She bounces the baby mercilessly.)* There! That ought to do it! PIG!
ALICE. I don't like to interfere...

DUCHESS. Piggy pig pig!
   Dance me a jig!
   Pour on molasses,
   And call it a wig! *(Sneezes.)*

ALICE. Bless you! *(ALICE sneezes.)* Bless me!

DUCHESS. What a terrible conversationalist you are, and that's a fact. Try the soup.

ALICE. The soup? Oh, all right. *(COOK sneezes.)* Bless you. *(DUCHESS snorts.)* Blessing people after they sneeze is a form of good manners.

COOK, DUCHESS, CAT (together). Do tell.

ALICE *(trying to be pleasant).* There may be too much pepper in the soup. *(COOK, insulted, shrieks and runs out with a metallic crash to punctuate her exit. ALICE watches her go then notices the CAT on the coat rack. He chuckles and grins.)* Gracious! What an unusual pussycat. Are you smiling, Kitty? *(CAT chuckles.)*

DUCHESS. It's not a smile, it's more of a grin. PIG!

ALICE. Pig? Please, are you addressing the cat or the baby or me?

DUCHESS *(for an answer, tosses the BABY in the air).* Pig! Pig! Piggy! Pig! Pig!

ALICE. Oh. Please don't think me forward, but is there a reason for the cat to grin like that?

DUCHESS. Certainly. He's a Cheshire Cat and that's why.

ALICE. Really?

DUCHESS. I said it, so it's so.

ALICE. Dinah doesn't grin.

DUCHESS. That's her problem.

ALICE. But Dinah's a cat, too, my cat, my dear little kittypuss. *(Another horrible crash off at right.)* And frankly, I'm wondering how I can get back home and see her right now.

DUCHESS. Stop wondering. If you were living backwards like me, you'd be home last Wednesday.

ALICE. But I'm not living backwards. I'm living forwards.

DUCHESS. The mess people make of their lives. But there's no time for tea. *(This is said as if ALICE had asked for tea.)*

ALICE. I didn't ask for tea.

DUCHESS. I expect I'll need white gloves and a fan.

ALICE. Oh, yes, that's right. I wonder, Your Highness, if you could tell me how to get to the Queen's croquet game?

DUCHESS. Certainly. I could tell you. But then I could choose not to tell you. You see my position?

(COOK enters, rushes to stove and bangs pots and pans mercilessly.)

ALICE. Do you think the Queen will object to my company?

DUCHESS. Nothing to fret about even if she does. She'll only behead you.

ALICE *(crossing to DUCHESS)*. Only?

DUCHESS. Tell you what. We'll make a game of it! After she has you beheaded, I'll box her ears. There, now, won't that be fun?

ALICE. No.

DUCHESS. There are two things I can't abide, and the other one is rudeness.

ALICE. Forgive me, I don't wish to seem rude, nor do I wish to be beheaded.

DUCHESS *(leaping up)*. Run! We've got to run! Quickly! Run! *(COOK, holding pots and pans, and DUCHESS, holding baby, run to apron. ALICE follows after being given a couple of pots to carry.)* Faster! Faster! No talking or singing or arithmetic! Run! *(As ALICE loses ground, COOK and DUCHESS stop and resume positions.)*

ALICE *(panting)*. I don't believe we got anywhere.

DUCHESS. Of course not!

ALICE. We're in exactly the same place.

DUCHESS. Thank heavens!

ALICE. But so is the cat and he didn't run. He didn't even get up.

DUCHESS *(leaping up and tossing baby to ALICE)*. Here! I must ready myself for the Queen's croquet game! *(As DUCHESS runs out L, COOK searches wildly for something to hit her with. After DUCHESS has passed, COOK swings at the air with a pot, then throws it after her, picks up another pot and runs off L. CAT vanishes behind his curtain.)*

ALICE. Well, I never! They might have said "good-bye."

(CAT reappears by opening the curtain in front of his shelf. COOK and DUCHESS run on and crowd around ALICE and say "Bye-bye" and then disappear off R, COOK chasing the DUCHESS.)

ALICE. Whatever am I to do with this dear little baby? *(BABY cries.)* There, there! I certainly shan't treat you as roughly as the Duchess did. *(He cries horribly, then the cries change gradually to oinks.)* Now, now! Rock-a-bye-baby...what a strange looking child. *(She is un-*

snapping its dress.) I do believe he somewhat resembles a...*(Oinks are quite discernible as such.)*...PIG!

(SEVEN runs on from L, attaches dog leash to PIG and pulls it off L as RABBIT runs on from R.)

RABBIT. There you are! Don't bother to explain, there isn't time! Just make certain you fetch my white gloves and fan and meet me on the dot. And remember, Mary Ann, there is absolutely no time for a haircut! *(He exits L with BABY's dress.)*

ALICE. I think I need a little help.

CAT *(opening his curtain)*. Tell me what happened to the baby?

ALICE *(crosses to CAT)*. It turned into a pig.

CAT. I thought it would. Are you having a good time?

ALICE. I'm a little confused. Between smiling and frowning sort of.

CAT. What's a dog do when he's happy?

ALICE. Wags his tail.

CAT. And when he's angry?

ALICE. He growls.

CAT. Now you take me. I wag my tail when I'm angry and growl when I'm happy.

ALICE. I call that purring.

CAT. Call it what you like. It's all part of the nice madness.

ALICE. I *am* having a good time. It's all so...unusual.

CAT. That's what you said you wanted, you know—something unusual to happen.

ALICE. Yes, I did. You heard that?

CAT. Are you going to play croquet with the Queen?

ALICE. I think so.

CAT. Good. I'll see you there. Or perhaps you'll see me there. You never know.

ALICE. It's all one and the same. That's the rule.

CAT. You're catching on.

ALICE. I'm trying.

CAT. By the way, did you say the baby changed into a fig?

ALICE. No, I said "pig."

CAT. I knew it was one or the other. *(Looking up.)* In that direction lives a Hatter and *(Looking down.)* in that direction lives a March Hare. Maybe one of them can help you. They're both mad, you know. *(He vanishes.)*

ALICE. Well, I expect the only thing to do now is...run! Faster and faster!

(As ALICE runs in place, the kitchen set is struck and the tea party is set up. See Production Note #3. Before the scene change is completed, ALICE stops running and speaks.)

ALICE. Oh dear! I'm so tired, I've just got to sit down for a while.

(THIRTEEN places stool behind her; she sits.)

ALL *(they are lined up along tea party table. Each says one word)*. And—how—long—pray—tell—do—you—intend—to—rest?

ALICE. Oh, I'd say about ten minutes. *(The ACTORS sigh and pose with folded arms to wait as the curtain falls.)*

END OF ACT ONE

ACT TWO

AT RISE: *The stage is set exactly as it was at the end of Act One. The ACTORS lean toward ALICE, sitting on stool, and speak in unison.*

ALL. Now?
ALICE. Now.

(THIRTEEN, now the DORMOUSE, retrieves stool and the set change is completed. As HATTER, MARCH HARE and DORMOUSE take their places at the table, ALICE speaks.)

ALICE. Well, now! I must have run especially fast...it seems I got to a tea party!
HATTER *(singing very fast and with practically no tune)*.
   Tea and crumpets
   Love 'em hot and cold
   Gongs and trumpets
   Take 'em young or old.
   Tea and crumpets
   Love 'em cold or hot,
   Gongs and trumpets
   Throw 'em in the pot.
   Oh, fiddle, fiddle, fiddle
   And a fiddle-dee-dee

>   Pass the bread and butter
>   And the marmalade to me!

HARE *(applauding)*. That's very nice, except for the tune and words.

HATTER. Thank you! Thank you! Encore!
   (Singing.)
>   Tea and crumpets…
   (Sees ALICE approaching the table. Speaks.)
>   Look! Look!
   (HATTER and HARE rise and motion her away.)

HATTER and HARE. No room! No room! No room!

DORMOUSE. No roooommm…*(They push his head down.)*

ALICE. Of course there's room. There's plenty of room. Look at all the places. I'll sit here. *(She sits on armchair at head of table.)*

HARE *(sitting)*. Have some ice cream.

ALICE. I…I don't see any ice cream.

HARE. There isn't any. *(Laughs hysterically.)*

ALICE. Then it wasn't very polite of you to offer me some.

HARE. And it wasn't very polite of you to sit down without being asked! *(HATTER laughs hysterically.)*

ALICE. The idea! Besides, I didn't know it was your table. It's set for so many places.

HARE. Easy come, easy went.

HATTER *(gasps)*. Your hair wants cutting.

ALICE. People here don't seem to realize that personal remarks are rude.

HATTER. I can give you a haircut and the Dormouse a shave in less time than it takes to say "Three thistles threw their thistle-down through thirty thick thermometers." *(HATTER takes a shaving brush from his hat and dips it in the icing of a cake and starts to brush it on*

DORMOUSE. DORMOUSE grabs brush and licks icing from it. Then he starts to tie a napkin around ALICE's neck. She throws it on the table. HARE sharpens knives.)

ALICE. I don't want a haircut, thank you!

DORMOUSE. You're welcome, I'm sure. *(HATTER and HARE sit.)*

HATTER. Why is a thistle like a thermometer? *(Looking at his watch.)* Quickly! *(HARE moves his head back and forth making clock sounds.)*

ALICE. Oh, good! Riddles! I love riddles!

HARE. I love riddles!

ALICE. Now let's see.

HARE. Now let's see.

ALICE. Why is a thistle like a thermometer?

HARE. We just had that riddle. Think up a new one.

ALICE. I'm trying to find the answer to *his* riddle.

HARE *(panic stricken)*. Where did you lose it?

ALICE. I didn't lose it. I haven't found it yet.

HARE *(frantic)*. Look in all the teacups.

DORMOUSE. No room! *(They push his head down.)*

HATTER. Stop talking in riddles and have some more tea.

ALICE. I can't have more when I haven't had any.

HATTER. Full already?

ALICE *(playing the game)*. No. More tea, please.

HARE. Splendid! *(ALICE extends her cup. HARE pours tea in HATTER's cup, DORMOUSE's mouth, and his own cup. When his cup is "filled," he drinks it and ALICE holds her cup under the still-tipped teapot.)*

HATTER *(gasps, runs around the table and kneels at ALICE's chair as HARE rises and stands over her)*. Have you thought of the answer yet?

ALICE. I'm afraid I don't know very much about thistles or thermometers. Tell me, what's the answer?

HATTER. I don't know. *(To HARE.)* Do you?

HARE. Haven't the faintest idea.

DORMOUSE. Me, either. *(HARE and HATTER, thinking this statement is the answer, clap and scream and resume positions.)*

ALICE. Really! Wasting time making up riddles that don't have any answers! *(ALL move down one place, including ALICE.)*

HARE. Everybody got a clean cup except the three of us.

HATTER. Last March, just before he went mad *(Points to HARE who giggles.)* I was performing at a great concert given by the Queen. I have a superb singing voice, you know. I was singing a lovely song: *(As HATTER sings, HARE strums on DORMOUSE's hands and makes "harp" sounds as he does.)*

    Twinkle, twinkle, little bat,

    How I wonder what you're at.

(Speaks.) Perhaps you know it?

ALICE. Sounds familiar.

HATTER. It goes on, you know, like this: *(Sings.)*

    Up above the world you fly

    Like a tea tray in the sky.

    Twinkle, twinkle, twinkle...

(HARE and DORMOUSE join in the "twinkles," each saying it as fast as he can. HATTER ends it by shouting one last "TWINKLE." Speaks.)

    I vote the Dormouse tells us a story!

HARE. I second and third the motion!

HATTER. Motion passed.

ALICE. That would be nice.

HARE. He's asleep. Hold your breath and count up to zero! *(They wake DORMOUSE and lift him on his stool.)*

DORMOUSE. Once upon a time there were three little sisters whose names were Elsie, Lacie and Tillie.
ALICE. Where did they live?
HARE and HATTER. Shh!
DORMOUSE. Stop interrupting! They lived, if you must know, at the bottom of a well. In fact, they lived happily ever after. *(He sits, sleeps.)*
ALICE *(after a moment)*. Is that all there is to the story?
HATTER. Of course not! That's the way all his stories begin. *(They stand DORMOUSE on the stool again.)*
DORMOUSE. After they lived happily ever after, all sorts of terrible things happened. Elsie and Tillie caught nasty colds and Lacie pricked her finger with a pin. *(HATTER and HARE cry loudly, but tears soon turn to cheers and applause.)*
HATTER. That's the best story I ever heard.
HARE. I'm glad it didn't get too complicated.
DORMOUSE. Here's another story. *(Overcome with ecstasy, HATTER and HARE fairly faint behind table. DORMOUSE narrates as though they were still sitting on stools.)* Once upon a time there were three sisters whose names were Elsie, Lacie and Tillie and they lived at the bottom of a well.
HATTER. Uh oh! Sounds like a good one.
HARE. They keep getting better.
DORMOUSE. And they took to drawing things. *(Joins them behind table.)*
HARE and HATTER. Drawing things.
ALICE. What for example?
DORMOUSE. Water, for example! They lived at the bottom of a well and they drew water!
ALICE. Oh, I see. A joke! A rather mild joke, actually.
HATTER. Listen to her! *(They do.)*

ALICE. Tell the truth I don't think the Dormouse's stories are...well, what shall I say? *(The THREE scream horribly. DORMOUSE faints into arms of HATTER.)*
HATTER. For one thing you can't say mouse's, you have to say mice. It's the *Dormice* stories. Learn the proper way.

(RABBIT enters R.)

RABBIT. Oh, there you are! Really, Mary Ann! The croquet game is scheduled to begin any moment now. Luckily I found you on the dot. My white gloves, please. *(HARE takes them out of teapot and hands them to ALICE who gives them to RABBIT.)* Good girl! Now, my fan. *(HATTER takes fan off his hat, passes it to ALICE, who gives it to RABBIT.)* Splendid! I'm going to recommend you for promotion. I'll even put in a good word with the Queen! It's the beginning of a great career! Just keep your head about you.
HARE, DORMOUSE and HATTER. Hurry!
RABBIT. To the croquet game!
ALICE. To the croquet game! Faster!

(They run off L and the scene is set for the game. TWO OF HEARTS and SEVEN OF HEARTS take positions at opposite ends of picket fence. See Production Note #4.)

TWO. Make way for her majesty, the Queen of...
SEVEN. Wait a minute! Are all the roses red?
TWO. The red ones are.
SEVEN *(spying white rose DR)*. Look!
TWO. Where?
SEVEN. There! A white rose! She'll cut off our heads!

(ALICE runs on alone from L and stands behind fence.)

TWO. Get the paint!

SEVEN. Where is it? *(They begin a frantic search for the paint, ad libbing, "Where is the paint!" ALICE, seeing it behind the fence, picks it up and hands it to TWO. They cross to white rose.)*

TWO. We haven't time to paint it properly.

SEVEN. Dip it in the paint can. She'll never notice.

TWO. Don't we hope. *(They dip the white rose in the can as ALICE crosses to them.)*

ALICE. Uh...*(They nearly faint with fright.)*

TWO. You startled us!

SEVEN. I nearly dropped the can!

TWO. Look, we haven't time for conversations.

ALICE. I was just wondering, why can't you leave the white rose the way it is?

TWO. We're fond of our heads, that's why!

SEVEN. It's the only head I have, see.

ALICE. What's that got to do with the white rose?

TWO. Everything!

SEVEN. Quickly, the paint. Dip the rose. Don't get any on your hands. And don't spill any. She'll spot it in a minute.

ALICE. You mean the Queen?

SEVEN. Who else?

ALICE. Wouldn't it be funny if she sniffed it and got red paint all over her nose?

TWO. Hilarious. *(They put white rose in can and pull out previously placed red rose.)*

SEVEN. There. *(TWO takes paint can off R and they resume positions to announce the QUEEN.)*

Act II ALICE IN WONDERLAND Page 33

TWO. Make way for their majesties, the King and Queen of Hearts! Bow! And stay that way!

ALICE. If I stay bowed, I'd never see them. What's the sense of coming here if I can't see them?

(Music rises. KING, QUEEN and KNAVE enter L, followed by RABBIT. KNAVE carries a crown on a velvet pillow. They parade about and finally stop. All moves are done in quick mechanical steps. Music out.)

QUEEN *(looking at ALICE)*. Who are you?

ALICE. If it pleases Your Majesties, I'm Alice.

QUEEN. It doesn't please me. Nothing pleases me! I'm in a constant state of displeasure. I like it that way. *(TWO and SEVEN clap hands and make p-p-p-p-p vocal sound.)* Who are they? *(They quake with fear.)*

ALICE. I'm sure I don't know.

QUEEN. Why not?

ALICE. Perhaps it's none of my business.

QUEEN *(enraged)*. Are you being impertinent? *(RABBIT crosses to between them.)*

ALICE. No, Your Majesty, I'm being Alice.

RABBIT *(feeling her forehead)*. She has a fever.

QUEEN. Well, I know a quick cure for a fever. *(ALL put fingers in ears as QUEEN shouts.)* OFF WITH HER HEAD!!

ALICE. You wouldn't dare. *(ALL gasp.)*

QUEEN *(this is too much)*. WHAAA-A-A-A-T??!!

KING. Please, dear, she's just a little girl.

QUEEN. She'll be a headless little girl if she doesn't mind her manners.

KING. Mind your manners. Do you mind?

ALICE. I don't mind. *(ALL sigh.)*

QUEEN. Do you play croquet?
ALICE. Yes, indeed. One of my favorite games.
QUEEN. I invented it! Ask them.
KING. She invented it.
RABBIT. She invented it.
TWO and SEVEN. She invented it! *(ALL look at KNAVE.)*
QUEEN. Ask the Knave of Hearts if you don't believe them.
KNAVE. Oh yes, she invented it.
RABBIT. And where would we be without it? *(QUEEN claps hands. ALL move about, reciting multiplication tables very rapidly.)*
QUEEN. Cease! *(They do.)* Prepare for the croquet game!

(ALL but ALICE huddle together in a mass which moves about as one body, while they make "beep-beep" sounds. Soon the RABBIT jumps out of the body and the others exit L.)

RABBIT. Have you seen Mary Ann?
ALICE. No. Have you?
RABBIT. Be sure and tell her the Duchess is in prison.
ALICE. What for?
RABBIT. She'll want to know.
ALICE. No, I mean, why is the Duchess in prison?
RABBIT. She was late arriving. That was bad enough, but then she went and boxed the Queen's ears, which was worse.
ALICE. I can imagine.
RABBIT. The Queen will probably have her beheaded.
ALICE *(mock serious)*. I'm rather surprised there's anyone left.

(KING, QUEEN, KNAVE, TWO and SEVEN enter L. TWO, SEVEN and QUEEN carry flamingos, exaggerated stuffed toys. KNAVE has a similar hedgehog. They ALL repeat everything the QUEEN says.)

QUEEN. Croquet! Time for the Croquet Game! On the double! Obey the rules! Wickets and mallets and players take heed!

(The game commences. TWO and SEVEN become the wickets. QUEEN makes several efforts to hit hedgehog with flamingo, but fails. She strikes TWO with flamingo, thinking he has stolen hedgehog. It in no conceivable way should resemble a croquet game. Finally, ALICE picks up hedgehog, runs left with it, and OTHERS line up across stage. The line behaves like a bullwhip with ALICE holding handle. ALICE passes hedgehog down the line. Eventually ALICE holds all three flamingos and the hedgehog. The OTHERS take them from her and exit L. Vocal beeps through all the preceding except bullwhip business. After their exit, CAT appears from behind picket fence where he has been hiding.)

CAT. You said you wanted something unusual to happen, remember? Is this unusual enough?
ALICE *(crossing to him)*. It's almost too unusual. I've never experienced such a croquet game. I can't quite believe the Queen invented it. She doesn't seem acquainted with any rules at all.
CAT. She isn't. She dismissed them long ago, even *before* she became acquainted with them.
ALICE. Did you hear about the Duchess?
CAT. Her head gone?

ALICE. No, but almost. She boxed the Queen's ears. Imagine! *(Pause.)* Don't you think we'd better do something about her?
CAT. Who?
ALICE. The Duchess.

(DUCHESS enters R.)

DUCHESS. There you are! My dear child. I've looked everywhere! Where have you been?
CAT. Get them to show you the Mock Turtle.
DUCHESS. Oh, yes, you mustn't miss that. Most people feel it's the high point of the trip.
ALICE. I thought you were under arrest for boxing the Queen's ears.
DUCHESS. Just a rumor.
CAT. Maybe the Mock Turtle will tell *you* his story. He's never told me. I don't think he's ever told anyone, come to think of it. *(Gasps.)* Uh oh. Here comes the Queen!
ALICE. Oh, dear!
DUCHESS. What's the matter?
ALICE. The Queen's coming.
DUCHESS. So I heard.
ALICE. Well, aren't you frightened?
DUCHESS. Not a bit. Not one little bit.
QUEEN *(off left)*. OFF WITH HER HEAD!!!
DUCHESS. Changed my mind. Ta ta. *(Afraid, DUCHESS runs off UL.)*
CAT. As I was saying, I'm sure you'll find the Mock Turtle very interesting. *(He vanishes.)*

(QUEEN, KING, KNAVE, TWO, SEVEN, RABBIT and the DUCHESS enter from L in a body.)

QUEEN. Off with his head!
OTHERS. Off with his head!
QUEEN. Off with everyone's head!
OTHERS. Off with everyone's head!
QUEEN. Stop! *(They ALL stop.)* Go! *(They march around a bit and stop.)* I've got to bake some tarts. The reason being it's a summer's day.
KNAVE. Good. I love tarts.
QUEEN. It's quite doubtful if you'll get any. *(To ALICE.)* You!
ALICE. Me, Your Majesty?
QUEEN. Why don't you go visit the Mock Turtle? Fetch the Gryphon. He'll lead the way. *(TWO and SEVEN exit R.)*
KING. What kind of tarts are you going to make, dear?
QUEEN. Indeed I am!
KING. Splendid! My favorite.

(GRYPHON enters R.)

RABBIT. Here's the Gryphon. To lead the way. *(ALICE crosses to GRYPHON.)*
QUEEN. Light the oven! Time for tarts! Off we go! *(They exit L.)*
GRYPHON. Come along. We've got to run.
ALICE. I knew we would. I'm getting used to it. In fact, I'm getting used to everything. It all seems quite normal now.
GRYPHON. I've never heard of "normal." What's that?
ALICE. I've forgotten.

GRYPHON. Start running.
ALICE. What else.

(Three crates are set DL. MOCK TURTLE enters, sobbing.)

GRYPHON *(stops running)*. Listen! That's he! That's the old duffer himself.
ALICE. Such deep-felt sobs! My heart aches for him. What's his great sorrow?
GRYPHON. Hasn't got one. Just his fancy. Like the Queen. She fancies having everyone beheaded. People are taking to fancies more and more these days. Have you noticed?
ALICE. No, but I shall, first chance I get.
GRYPHON. Come on. *(They walk to the MOCK TURTLE.)* You got a visitor. A young lady, see? *(MOCK TURTLE sobs.)* She wants to hear your history. *(He sobs louder.)* Of course, if you don't feel up to it, maybe some other time. *(GRYPHON starts away.)*
MOCK TURTLE. Wait! She shall hear my history. All of it. Sit down, both of you, and please don't utter one word until I've finished. *(They sit. MOCK TURTLE sobs.)*
ALICE. How can he finish if he never starts?
GRYPHON and MOCK TURTLE. Shh!
MOCK TURTLE *(with great effort)*. Once, long ago, when everything was different, I was not a Mock Turtle. I was real. *(MOCK TURTLE sobs as GRYPHON shrieks.)*
ALICE. Well, I want to thank you for that interesting history.
GRYPHON and MOCK TURTLE. Shh!
MOCK TURTLE. We all went to school when we were little. We went to school every day. We called it day-school.

ALICE. That's not terribly unusual, you know. I go to school every day, too!

MOCK TURTLE. Do you study "extras"?

ALICE. French and music. They're extra.

MOCK TURTLE. We studied washing. Do you?

ALICE. No.

MOCK TURTLE. Doesn't sound like much of a school you've got there. How about teachers? My teacher was an old crab. Do you have an old crab for a teacher?

ALICE. Depends on her mood.

MOCK TURTLE. Odd. Tell me, have you spent much time under the sea?

ALICE. Not a great deal.

MOCK TURTLE. You've never met a lobster?

ALICE. No, but I do like them.

MOCK TURTLE. Yes, they can be most amusing, especially during the Lobster Quadrille.

ALICE. What's the Lobster Quadrille?

MOCK TURTLE. A dance, of course. We'll do it for you! If you insist.

ALICE. I insist. *(GRYPHON and MOCK TURTLE begin a lugubrious dance. Singing.)*
   Will you walk a little faster?
   Said a whiting to a snail...

ALICE. What's a whiting?

GRYPHON. A small fish.

MOCK TURTLE. There's a porpoise close behind us, and he's treading on my tail. See how eagerly the lobsters and the turtles all advance! They are waiting on the shingle. Will you come and join the dance?

GRYPHON. Will you, won't you, will you, won't you, will you join the dance? *(They sit.)*

MOCK TURTLE. Well now, you must tell us *your* history.

ALICE. *My* history? All of it?

MOCK TURTLE. No. Just begin at the beginning, go through to the end, then stop.

ALICE. Well.

MOCK TURTLE. We haven't got all day, you know. The trial will probably begin any moment now.

ALICE. The trial? What trial?

GRYPHON and MOCK TURTLE. "The Queen of Hearts, she made some tarts, All on a summer day...and so forth."

ALICE. Oh, yes! But why must there be a trial?

GRYPHON. To find the culprit, I expect. Besides, it's the rule. Better sing it now, quickly, before we have to go.

MOCK TURTLE. All right.

(Singing.)

    Soup, beautiful soup, so rich and green,
    Who for dainties would not stoop...

(RABBIT enters R.)

RABBIT. Hurry up! The trial's about to begin!

GRYPHON. Come on!

RABBIT. On to the trial! Hurry! The trial's about to begin! Follow me! *(RABBIT and GRYPHON run off R.)*

MOCK TURTLE *(to ALICE).* Better walk a little faster.

ALICE. I enjoyed hearing your history.

MOCK TURTLE *(bows).* Yours was pretty good, too. Nice and brief.

(Singing.)

    Soup of the evening, beaut-i-ful soup.

(As he exits, ALICE turns and runs in place and the setting changes to the trial scene. See Production Note #5. After setup, ALL ad lib until RABBIT shouts.)

RABBIT. Silence in the court! Silence in the court!

(Silence and ALICE joins the scene, enjoying it all.)

RABBIT. Ready, Your Majesties!
QUEEN. Where's the prisoner?
KNAVE. Here, Your Majesty.
QUEEN. Where's the jury?

(Six hand puppets present themselves in jury box. SEVEN, FOUR and TWELVE are the puppeteers.)

KING. Herald! We are ready! The accusation, Herald! Read it! *(Pause.)* HERALD!
RABBIT. My name isn't Harold.
KING. I know that! You're the Herald of the Court, so read the accusation!
RABBIT. I've got to blow my trumpet first. *(JURY laughs. RABBIT blows trumpet and unrolls a scroll from which he reads.)*
"The Queen of Hearts, she made some tarts,
All on a summer day.
The Knave of Hearts *(KNAVE moans.)*
He stole those tarts,
And took them quite away!"
KING. Call the first witness!
RABBIT. Call the first witness!
ALICE *(having fun)*. First witness, if you please!
QUEEN. Who is she?

KING. A little girl, my dear.

QUEEN. Well, she's liable to be a headless little girl if she doesn't mind her manners! So now you know!

(HATTER, the first witness, enters R. As he crosses to witness box, JURY ad libs greetings to him.)

HATTER *(holding a teacup and a slice of bread)*. First witness reporting for duty. *(He is very nervous.)*

QUEEN. What's that you've got there?

HATTER. A cup of bread and butter, and a piece of tea, Your Majesty.

QUEEN. A likely story.

RABBIT *(crossing to HATTER)*. State your name, address, occupation and complete history.

KING *(kindly)*. And try not to be nervous or I'll have you executed on the spot. *(JURY laughs.)* Take off your hat!

HATTER. Why? You want to buy it? I'm a hatter, you know. Or should or shouldn't.

QUEEN. What do you mean by that?

HATTER. I make hats.

QUEEN. Aha! *(JURY laughs.)*

HATTER. I make them to sell. So I can't take off my hat unless you buy it.

KING. Just give your evidence. And remember; if you shake, it's a sure sign you're guilty!

QUEEN. Did you see the prisoner steal my tarts?

HATTER. Who's the prisoner?

RABBIT. He is. The Knave of Hearts. *(KNAVE bows.)*

QUEEN. Well?

HATTER. No, Your Majesty, I didn't see him steal your tarts.

Act II   ALICE IN WONDERLAND   Page 43

QUEEN. Aha! *(JURY laughs.)* Why not?

HATTER. I was having my tea. *(He takes a bite out of the cup.)*

ALICE. He's absolutely right, you know. *(ALL gasp.)*

QUEEN. She's liable to be a headless little girl, as someone once remarked.

ALICE. I've never attended a trial before, but it seems to me this one isn't going quite as it should. *(To HATTER.)* You're sure you didn't see anyone steal the Queen's tarts?

HATTER. How could I? I'm always at a tea party.

ALICE. There.

KING *(looking around)*. Where?

ALICE. I mean, there, he doesn't know anything about the tarts.

RABBIT. She's trying to confuse everything! Besides, you're supposed to be home doing the dishes, Mary Ann.

ALICE. I'm not Mary Ann. *(ONE OF THE JURORS bites finger of RABBIT who squeals and scampers away.)*

QUEEN. Aha! *(JURY laughs.)* An impostor! If you're not Mary Ann, where is she?

ALICE. Mary Ann, I suppose, is home doing the dishes. Or getting a haircut. Now then, the Hatter knows nothing about the stolen tarts, so he's quite innocent and free to go. *(ALL gasp, mock shock.)*

HATTER. Thank you.

ALICE. Give my regards to the March Hare and the Dormouse, won't you?

HATTER. What about Elsie, Lacie and Tillie?

ALICE. Them, too.

QUEEN. Just remove his hat and head outside.

HATTER *(as he runs off)*. If you can catch me, which you can't! *(He's gone.)*
KING. Call the next witness!
RABBIT. Call the next witness!
ALICE. Next witness, please.

(COOK enters R, banging pots and pans. KNAVE runs L, RABBIT runs R, and JURY vanishes. When COOK is in the stand she taps lightly on one pot and the trial resumes.)

ALICE. State your...
RABBIT *(taking over)*. State your name, your address...
COOK. Wow! Wow! Wow!
RABBIT. State your name, your address...
COOK *(raising pot)*. Save your breath.
RABBIT *(tugging on QUEEN's skirt)*. Uh, I think perhaps one of Your Majesties should question this witness.
COOK. Don't give a hoot who questions me. Won't do any good.
KING. Now see here, my good woman...
COOK. Not me. FIGS!!! *(JURY laughs.)*
RABBIT. What were the tarts made of? You're a cook and you should know.
COOK. Mostly pepper.
KING. Members of the jury, consider your verdict.
RABBIT. Not yet! Not yet! Not nearly yet!
ALICE. If the tarts were stolen, what are they doing there?
KING. Stop confusing the jury! *(JURY giggles.)*
QUEEN. We'd get a lot more done around here if we chopped off everyone's head. And that's a fact.
ALICE *(to KNAVE)*. Did you steal the tarts?

KNAVE. I must have. The poem says so. "The Knave of Hearts, he stole the tarts..."
ALICE. Well, just because the poem says you stole the tarts doesn't necessarily make it true. I've heard poems that are not quite the truth. *(ALL gasp.)*
QUEEN. Name one!
ALICE. All right. "Twinkle, twinkle little bat, how I wonder what you're at!" Now, then, we all know that bats don't twinkle.
RABBIT. They squeak.
ALICE. Yes, but they don't twinkle.
QUEEN. I hate that poem, especially when it's sung.
ALICE. The point is: the poor Knave didn't steal the tarts just because the poem says so.
COOK. He doesn't twinkle, either. Needs more pepper! *(Starts out, turns back at exit.)* Everybody needs more pepper. *(She gestures as though tossing pepper. ALL sneeze. COOK exits and her exit is followed by an offstage crash.)*
RABBIT. One more witness!
KING. Call the last witness!
RABBIT. I call...Alice!
ALICE. Here!
RABBIT. Take the stand!
ALICE. All right! *(She does.)*
RABBIT. State your name, address, occupation and complete history.
ALICE. I think my name is Alice.
QUEEN. Aha! *(JURY giggles.)*
ALICE. And I used to live in a lovely white house. At least I did when I got up this morning. And I have a dear little kitty called Dinah.
KING *(to JURY)*. Make a note of that! *(They laugh.)*

ALICE. I suppose you might say my occupation is daydreaming. I do a great deal of it. And I think it would be great fun if we'd pass those tarts about and perhaps someone could make some tea.
RABBIT. She wants to destroy the evidence.
KING. Consider your verdict.
ALICE. I'm awfully hungry.
RABBIT. She's guilty! She's guilty! She practically admitted it!
ALICE. But I'm not on trial. The Knave of Hearts is. Do let's have a tart. I'm sure they're delicious.
QUEEN. Of course they are.
ALICE. Are they cherry?
QUEEN. Yes! Give the girl a tart.
RABBIT. But, Your Majesty...
QUEEN. Give her a tart or heads will roll! Give me one, too! *(RABBIT passes tarts around.)*
RABBIT. Here, Mary Ann. Try one.
ALICE. Thank you, little Dormouse.
RABBIT. I'm not the Dormouse!
ALICE. And I'm not Mary Ann.
RABBIT. Nonsense!
ALICE. Oh, I agree, it's sheer nonsense. Wondrous nonsense!
QUEEN *(chanting)*. Don't turn your nose up at nonsense, don't!
JURY. We won't! *(Repeated seven times in all, fast.)*
ALICE. If you turn your nose up at nonsense here...
QUEEN. You'll miss all the fun!
ALICE. The fun will be done!
QUEEN. Before you get going, the race will be won!
ALICE. And nobody cares for a gloomy, doomy grouch!

JURY. Ouch, ouch, ouch, ouch. Ouch, ouch, ouch, ouch. Ouch, ouch, ouch, ouch, *(Pause.)* OUCH!
QUEEN. It's the new rule: Never turn your nose up at nonsense! Not till bats twinkle. The Knave is free and that's the rule, too. *(ALL cheer.)*
KNAVE. How nice! I've been guilty every other time, you know.
ALICE. You've been on trial before?
KNAVE. Only when she makes some tarts, which is every afternoon. "The Queen of Hearts, she made some tarts, all on a summer day."
ALICE. But in winter...
KNAVE. Winter? It's always summer here.
ALICE. It is?
ALL. Yes. That's the rule.
ALICE. I should have guessed. Such a wondrous place. *(She sits on floor as at opening.)* I'll not soon forget it. Everyone will say I was daydreaming. Except Dinah. She'll believe me. I'll tell her how I followed a little White Rabbit who calls me Mary Ann, and then swam with a Mouse in a pool of tears. My own! Does sound a bit like a daydream. Never mind. Dinah will love it. The Hatter and the March Hare and that tea party that just goes on an on. Oh, yes, and the Duchess's baby who turned into a pig—that'll make Dinah laugh. Or at least smile. Like the Cheshire Cat. So much to remember. The Gryphon and the Mock Turtle and that very strange croquet game. Oh, and the trial, which I think I won, but you can't be too certain about anything in... in...funny, I don't even know what this place is called.
ALL *(softly)*. Wonderland!
ALICE. Of course. Wonderland. *(ALL sigh.)* Nice. *(She smiles and shuts her eyes.)*

ONE *(still gently)*. Isn't it incredible? We actually found a girl named Alice! Not necessary, of course, but a little added touch.

TWO. She seemed to enjoy everything, too.

THREE. So cooperative.

FOUR. And so, well, nice.

ALICE *(as though awakening)*. I *did* enjoy everything. Absolutely everything. *(ALL chuckle.)* I hope *everyone* gets a turn?

ONE. Possibly.

ALICE. Wonderland won't be too difficult for them to find, will it?

ONE. Like finding your nose in the dark. *(ALL elaborately extend an arm, squeeze their eyes shut, and slowly bring a pointed finger to their noses.)* See?

ALL *(eyes popped open and big smiles)*. Easy!

ALICE. Then, all you have to do is pretend?

ALL. That's it. *(The ACTORS begin backing towards the exits on stage and there is soft laughter.)*

ALICE. Just like a daydream. *(The ACTORS exit quietly and quickly. ALICE yawns and sighs happily.)* An unusual daydream. *(Smile, small laugh.)*

CURTAIN

PRODUCTION NOTES

1. Two actors take the placards and use them to form the sides of the opening. Two others stand in back of these sides on stools and hold a third section over the top. The others put a small crate or stool nearby with the piece of cake and bottle on it and then they gather behind the opening. (One actor gets a mouth full of water—or a water gun—to squirt out as the fountain, while the others get roses or flowers to hold up when she mentions the word "garden"). The "shrinking" and "growing" effects are done by having the actors holding the placards close them in or open them up. This idea of "suggesting" the action should be incorporated throughout the performance if possible.

2. The actors set up a stove, a stool for the DUCHESS who carries on the "baby" (actually a toy pig) and also a coat rack large enough for the CHESHIRE CAT to rest on the top shelf. There should be a draw-curtain in front of the shelf for the CAT to draw and "disappear."

3. The actors rush out and strike the kitchen scene. A long table on horses is brought on. The tablecloth appears to be part of the COOK's costume, wrapped around her several times. It is unwhirled by the others and spread over the table. Others set the teapots, cups, saucers, and cakes, a large armchair and several stools lined up on the upstage side.

4. To strike the long table, two actors unseen underneath it walk it off so it appears to be moving by itself. The garden consists of a picket fence (masked in the back so that the CAT can pop up unseen prior to his entrance) and the stools upside-down with red roses inserted in holes drilled in the legs.

5. We made six hand puppets (all animals) which were held by three actors hidden behind a simply-constructed puppet theatre. The witness box was indicated by replacing the picket fence section as three sides of a square. The KING and QUEEN sat on small ladders.

DIRECTOR'S NOTES

DIRECTOR'S NOTES

DIRECTOR'S NOTES

ര # DIRECTOR'S NOTES

DIRECTOR'S NOTES

DIRECTOR'S NOTES